DREAMWORKS

ABOMINABLE

PEARL

Yi's Journey Home

Adapted by May Nakamura
Illustrated by Mauricio Abril

SIMON SPOTLIGHT
An imprint of Simon & Schuster Children's Publishing Division
New York   London   Toronto   Sydney   New Delhi
1230 Avenue of the Americas, New York, New York 10020
This Simon Spotlight edition August 2019
© 2019 Universal Studios and Shanghai Pearl Studio Film and Television Technology Co. All Rights Reserved.
All rights reserved, including the right of reproduction in whole or in part in any form.
SIMON SPOTLIGHT and colophon are registered trademarks of Simon & Schuster, Inc.
For information about special discounts for bulk purchases, please contact Simon & Schuster Special Sales at
1-866-506-1949 or business@simonandschuster.com.
Manufactured in the United States of America 0719 LAK
2 4 6 8 10 9 7 5 3 1
ISBN 978-1-5344-5084-4
ISBN 978-1-5344-5085-1 (eBook)

Nice to meet you! I'm Yi. I live with my mom and NaiNai, which means "grandma" in Mandarin. Our home might be small, but it's always filled with laughter, my violin music, and a lot of pork buns. Yum!

I used to avoid being at home, though. That's because I missed my dad. The house felt lonely and empty without him.

Instead of spending time with my mom and NaiNai, I kept myself busy— really busy! I washed cars, walked dogs, fixed computers, babysat . . . anything that distracted me from thinking about my dad.

My secret fort was the only place that actually felt like "home." It was on our apartment building's rooftop, and I filled it with my favorite things, like my dad's violin and his postcard collection. I would spend my time looking at the postcards and daydreaming about visiting all those places someday.

Then one day, something extraordinary happened. I climbed up to my secret fort and found . . . a yeti! You know, those giant mythical creatures that live on Mount Everest? They actually exist!

What was a yeti doing in a big city? It turned out that he had been captured by some people who were clearly up to no good. The yeti was trying to escape and get home to his family. I let him hide in my fort, but then my neighbors Jin and Peng found him. And Jin called the police!

The yeti and I quickly climbed down off the roof, dashed through the city, and jumped on a boat to escape. Jin and Peng got caught in the chaos and ended up on the boat too.

"I guess we're coming with you, Everest!" I said to the yeti. I decided to call him Everest, just like his home.

During the boat ride, I mapped out our journey. We would cross the Yellow Mountain to get to the Yangtze River. Then we'd follow the river toward Mount Everest.

"Mount Everest? That has to be hundreds of miles away," said Jin.

"Actually, it's thousands," corrected Peng.

I didn't care how far away it was. I was determined to get Everest back home, safe and sound.

When we reached the Yellow Mountain, it was taller than anything I had ever seen. Lush trees and beautiful dandelions grew everywhere. It was breathtaking!

The vibrant scenery wasn't the only thing that took my breath away, though. We had to climb thousands of steps to cross the mountain. What a grueling workout!

We found our way to a fishing village along the Yangtze River. Guess who we ran into in the village? The people who had captured Everest! They started chasing us down the river. Our boat was fast, but their boat was even faster!

Then something magical happened. Everest started humming, his fur glowed blue, and our boat began to rise. Soon we were gliding over a canola-flower field! Thanks to Everest's extraordinary powers, we were able to escape.

When Everest stopped humming, we crash-landed into the field. I ran over to my violin case, but it was too late. My dad's postcards were scattered everywhere, the violin was cracked, and every string was broken.

I burst into tears. Every night, my dad used to play me the same song on the violin. Now that violin was broken, and I had never felt so distant from my family.

But then Everest used his magic to put the violin back together. The instrument was as good as new. No, it was even better than new!

And Jin helped me realize that I shouldn't give up on my family. I still had my mom and NaiNai . . . and *I* had been the one pushing them away.

Peng helped me pick up the postcards. "Yi, these are all the places we've been!" he said.

I gasped. The Yellow Mountain, the Yangtze River, the canola-flower fields . . . Peng was right. Our journey had taken us to the places from my dad's postcards!

We had visited every place but one: the Leshan Buddha. It was the place that my dad wanted me to see the most. When we arrived, I pulled out my violin and played the song that my dad had always played. All around me flowers began to bloom. The yeti hair that Everest had strung my violin with was magical.

After crossing more meadows, groves, and bridges, we finally reached Mount Everest. We had led Everest to safety!

It was hard to say goodbye, but I knew that Everest was happiest with his family. And I realized that I couldn't wait to see my family too.

When I arrived back home, I gave my mom and NaiNai a big hug. At last, I knew that my journey had led me to where I needed to be. Everest was home, and I was home!

I still miss my dad, and I miss Everest, too. But thinking about them doesn't make me sad anymore. Instead, it makes me happy to remember all the memories we shared together.

I love my family, and I'm so happy to be spending time with them again. In fact, now Jin and Peng sometimes come over for dinner—so you could even say that our family has grown!

It was all thanks to one magical yeti named Everest!